To May
with love

ORCHARD BOOKS
338 Euston Road, London NW1 3BH
Orchard Books Australia
Level 17/207 Kent Street, Sydney, NSW 2000

First published in 1999 by Orchard Books
First published in paperback in 2001
This edition published in 2009
ISBN 978 1 40830 341 2
Text and illustrations © Caroline Uff 1999

The right of Caroline Uff to be identified as the author and illustrator of this work
has been asserted by her in accordance with the Copyright, Designs and Patents Act, 1988.
A CIP catalogue record for this book is available from the British Library.

1 3 5 7 9 10 8 6 4 2

Printed in China

Orchard Books is a division of Hachette Children's Books, an Hachette Livre UK company.
www.hachettelivre.co.uk

Hello Lulu

Caroline Uff

ORCHARD BOOKS

This is Lulu.

Hello
Lulu.

This is Lulu's house.
"Come in!"
says Lulu.

This is Lulu's Mummy

and this is Lulu's
Daddy.

This is Lulu's baby brother.

He can say lu-lu lu-lu.

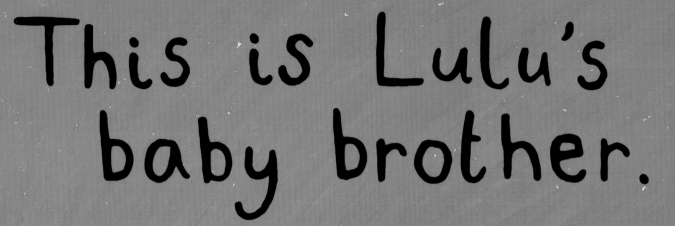

This is Lulu's big sister. She goes to big school.

This is Lulu's Teddy.

One of his ears is a bit wobbly.

Lulu kisses him better.

Look at Lulu's new shoes!

Red is Lulu's favourite colour.

Lulu's dog likes biscuits.

This is
Lulu's best friend.

This is Lulu's Granny.

Lulu likes teatime at Granny's house.

But best of all
Lulu loves her family
and they all love her.

Bye bye
Lulu!